Dear Parents:

Congratulations! Your child is taking
the first steps on an exciting journey.
The destination? Independent reading!

STEP INTO READING® will help your child get there. The program offers
five steps to reading success. Each step includes fun stories and colorful
art or photographs. In addition to original fiction and books with favorite
characters, there are Step into Reading Non-Fiction Readers, Phonics Readers
and Boxed Sets, Sticker Readers, and Comic Readers—a complete literacy
program with something to interest every child.

Learning to Read, Step by Step!

Ready to Read   Preschool–Kindergarten
• big type and easy words • rhyme and rhythm • picture clues
For children who know the alphabet and are eager to
begin reading.

Reading with Help   Preschool–Grade 1
• basic vocabulary • short sentences • simple stories
For children who recognize familiar words and sound out
new words with help.

Reading on Your Own   Grades 1–3
• engaging characters • easy-to-follow plots • popular topics
For children who are ready to read on their own.

Reading Paragraphs   Grades 2–3
• challenging vocabulary • short paragraphs • exciting stories
For newly independent readers who read simple sentences
with confidence.

Ready for Chapters   Grades 2–4
• chapters • longer paragraphs • full-color art
For children who want to take the plunge into chapter books
but still like colorful pictures.

STEP INTO READING® is designed to give every child a successful
reading experience. The grade levels are only guides; children will progress
through the steps at their own speed, developing confidence in their reading.

Remember, a lifetime love of reading starts with a single step!

Visit us on the Web!
StepIntoReading.com
rhcbooks.com

Educators and librarians, for a variety of teaching tools, visit us at RHTeachersLibrarians.com

ISBN 978-0-593-38243-1 (trade) — ISBN 978-0-593-38244-8 (lib. bdg.)
ISBN 978-0-593-38245-5 (ebook)

Printed in the United States of America

10 9 8 7 6 5 4 3 2 1

WAFFLES + MOCHI™

PICKLE PARTY!

by Frank Berrios

based on the Netflix original
series *Waffles + Mochi*, created by
Erika Thormahlen & Jeremy Konner

illustrated by Sarah Rebar

Random House 🏠 New York

This is Waffles.

This is Mochi.

They are best friends!

They work
at the supermarket.

Oops!
Waffles drops
the last jar
of pickles.

Kennedy cannot wait
for her birthday.
She really wants
pickles at her party!

She is sad.

Waffles and Mochi
must find
a pickle plant—fast!

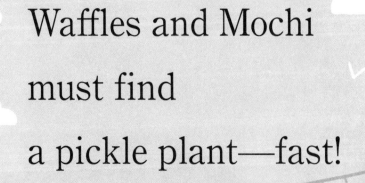

"You need to *make*
a pickle," says Busy.
"Pickles do not
grow on plants."

Another friend helps
Waffles and Mochi learn
how to pickle fruits
and vegetables.

They place salt,
water, vinegar,
and spices
in a jar.

They pickle carrots
and mangoes!

They pickle yummy
olives and cucumbers!

Oof!

Oh, no!

Waffles and Mochi learn

that it takes five days

for cucumbers

to become pickles.

They must wait.

So they wait . . .

and wait . . .

and wait some more.

After five long days,

the pickles are ready!

Waffles and Mochi

race to Kennedy's party!

Kennedy smiles.

She loves her present!

Good things come
to those who wait.
Pickles and birthdays
are very good things!

Thanks to
Waffles and Mochi,
the party is perfect.
And the pickles
are yummy, too!